P9-DXS-589

Someplace to Go

Maria Testa
Illustrated by **Karen Ritz**

Albert Whitman & Company
Morton Grove, Illinois

The text is set in Janson.
Illustrations were rendered in watercolor.
Design is by Herman Adler Design Group.

Library of Congress Cataloging-in-Publication Data

Testa, Maria.
　Someplace to go / written by Maria Testa; illustrated by Karen
Ritz.
　　　p. cm.
　Summary: Davey describes how he spends his time after school
trying to keep safe and warm until he can meet his mother and older
brother when the shelter opens at eight o'clock.
　ISBN 0-8075-7524-0
　[1. Homeless persons—Fiction.] I. Ritz, Karen, ill. II. Title.
PZ7.T2877So　1996　　　　　　　　　　　　95-32022
[E]—dc20　　　　　　　　　　　　　　　　　CIP
　　　　　　　　　　　　　　　　　　　　AC

Text copyright © 1996 by Maria Testa. Illustrations copyright © 1996
by Karen Ritz. Published in 1996 by Albert Whitman & Company,
6340 Oakton Street, Morton Grove, Illinois 60053. Published
simultaneously in Canada by General Publishing, Limited, Toronto.

For Antonio, my love.

MT

M s. Perez stands next to her desk and tells us to stay in our seats. "Wait for the final bell," she says, like she always does every day. When the bell rings, all the kids grab their books and jump up because they just can't wait to go home. All the kids except me. Seems like a long time since I had someplace to go after the final bell.

Out in the hallway, everyone's running. My friend Josh throws his soccer ball to me.

"Hey, Davey," he says. "You want to play awhile until my mom gets here?" Sometimes Josh's mom is late, but she always picks him up in her little blue car, and she always looks happy.

I tell Josh that soccer sounds fine to me.

It's freezing outside. Most everyone else is playing basketball, but Josh likes soccer better. I don't care. I'll play anything as long as I can keep moving enough to stay warm.

Pretty soon, Josh's mom drives up, smiling and beeping her horn. She asks me if I need a ride home, and I say no, thank you. I watch them drive away, and I want to call after them that it's okay; someday soon I'll have a place to go, and then my mom will smile a lot, too.

I start walking. When you're all alone, it's better to be walking than to be standing still. Standing still gets you noticed when you might not want to be. That's what my brother, Anthony, says and he should know, being almost sixteen.

Anthony's out looking for a job. If he gets one, and Mom keeps her new job at the hospital laundry, then maybe we can get a place again.

I miss our old apartment, the one we had before the paper mill closed almost two years ago and Mom lost her job. Mom worked at the mill for most of her life, but she says she likes her new job better, anyway.

I've got a job, too. My job is to do well in school and stay out of trouble every day until eight o'clock when the shelter opens. That's when we can all be together. So I keep on walking.

Zack's Market over on Pine Street is a good place to stop for a break. It's warm inside. Zack says hi to me because he knows I never once tried to steal anything from his store, not ever. Lots of people steal from Zack, and it puts him in a bad mood.

I walk up and down the aisles, looking at all the shelves full of food.

Once, Zack gave me an apple, for free. I'm hoping he'll give me another one today, but he doesn't. The soup kitchen won't open for hours. I wish Zack wasn't always in such a bad mood.

I leave Zack's and walk to the public library. It's warm there, too.

My social studies class is working on a project about prehistoric people. I find a book and read about hunters and gatherers. Some people used to gather everything they needed to live right from the land around them. They didn't need money.

I imagine myself in Zack's store, taking all the apples I can carry. "I'm a gatherer," I'd say.

I read for a long time, and then suddenly I'm not reading anymore and there's a man waking me up. He's wearing a gold badge that flashes in my eyes.

"I'm sorry," he says. "You're not allowed to sleep in here."

I get really hot, and I jump up and walk away fast from that man and everyone else who saw me fall asleep. Then I start running and don't stop until I'm back out on the street.

The wind swirls around me, and I shiver even though I was sweating a minute ago. The clock above the library says it's only a little after five. The soup kitchen won't open until six. I hope Anthony's there—I don't like eating alone.

I start walking again, pretending I'm a gatherer. I look everywhere for things to gather. I don't find anything good, but I keep hoping.

I'm daydreaming, and the next thing I know I'm staring at three big guys in a doorway and they're staring right back at me. I don't see much, just a couple of plastic bags, but that's enough. I've seen drugs before.

I used to have another brother, Michael, ten years older than me. I didn't know him too well, and then he got killed. Some people say he was like those guys in the doorway, dealing drugs, but Mom says don't you believe it.

One of the guys steps out. He smiles at me. I don't smile back. I want to shout at him, instead.

Hey, did you know my brother?
Hey, did you kill my brother?

But I know better and don't say anything.

"Keep on walking, little man," the smiling guy says, and I do.

I don't know where else to go, so I walk to the soup kitchen, even though it's too early. The line outside is already long. I run alongside it, back and forth, looking for Anthony, but he's not there.

I stand at the end of the line, missing Anthony and missing Mom and wishing I could stop shivering.

I eat alone.

It's nice and warm inside, and the food is pretty good. I'm sitting at the end of a long table, next to a family with so many kids, no one even notices me except the baby. She smiles at me. I smile back and try to pretend that I'm really her big brother. It doesn't work. I know I don't belong.

I get up from the table as soon as I finish eating. The people who run the soup kitchen don't mind if you stick around for a while as long as you give up your seat for the next person. I hang out near the doorway until the place closes down and I have to leave.

It's pitch black outside. I walk near the curb, under the streetlights, heading toward the shelter. I hear footsteps, fast, like someone's running, and I whip around, almost scared.

And then there's Anthony, right in front of me. He hugs me big and picks me up off the ground.

"I got a job!" he says, and his voice sounds like singing.

We walk to the shelter together, and I don't mind the cold or the dark. Anthony says that flipping burgers is just fine, everyone starts somewhere. He throws his arm around my shoulders.

"How's school?" he asks.

"OK," I say.

"Things are getting better, Davey," he says, and I believe him.

Mom's waiting for us in the lobby at the shelter.
She hugs us both like she never wants to let us go.

We stand in line, waiting to check in, and Mom
asks about our day. Anthony says he got a job and I
say my day went fine and Mom closes her eyes, tired
but happy. She smiles a smile that's just like home.

Maria Testa is a graduate of Yale University Law School. She is primarily interested in the law as it affects women, children, and the poor, and her background includes work in the areas of housing law, domestic violence, and criminal defense/post-conviction advocacy. She is the author of several books for young people, including *Thumbs Up, Rico!* Maria lives in Portland, Maine, with her husband and son.

Karen Ritz has a bachelor's degree in children's literature from the University of Minnesota. She teaches illustration at the college level and frequently speaks to elementary school children about book illustration. She has illustrated many books for children, including *A Family That Fights*.